Here is the story of Georgia Bear,
Passed down from parents to children with care.
He was the captain of a taxi boat,

He sailed the water and told funny jokes.
Generations of Bears enlightened,
By the lesson he learned on Jekyll Island.

Georgia Bear was just doing his job,
When he picked up a small group of hogs.
The Pigs spoke of more than the barn,
They desired to take over the farm.
A toast and their glasses went clank,
They aimed to take over the Piggy Bank.

The farm animals had always traded
paper called money,
And they backed it with Golden Bee
harvested honey.
One piece of paper represented one gold
honey pound,
Money for honey so the paper was
sound.
Ten pieces of paper was easy to hold,
And was the same as ten pounds of bee
honey gold.

Together the Pigs forged a master plan,
To separate money from honey and put control in their hands.
They would tell the animals they could all have more money,
If the pigs could do a trick that was funny.
"We will print more and more money, as much as we need,"
"Think of all the animals we will be able to feed."

Printing more money comes with one tiny catch,
It limits the amount of gold honey you get.
In the past it was one piece of paper for one pound of gold,
Now your money's worth less as you start to grow old.
One piece of paper, no, we will need two or three,
For one pound of honey worked by a bee.

It wasn't long until the pigs
plan was achieved,
And they still had another
scheme up their sleeve.

"Come animals take money, it's free,"
"Well it's free but it does come with a fee."
"We will give you all of the money you request,"
"All you must do is pay us back with interest."
"Want ten pieces of paper? Sure, just pay us back twelve,"
"Anything you need, you can buy it yourself."

Sloth took some money
just to go lay around,
Worm took some money
for a big home
underground.
"A chipmunks house has to
be nicer than worms,"
So he filled his home with
lights, stones, and
diamond filled urns.

Cow bought enough grass to eat
till he dropped,
And Rooster took chickens
to the store to shop.

Lions refused to move or to leave,
Even after they watched their water recede.
Red fox didn't care what anyone did,
As long as he could get back at the pigs.
Only one animal resisted temptation, desires, and dreams,
The Bears decided to live within their means.

The Bears built their homes with blood, sweat, and tears,
With grind, they crushed, and conquered their fears.
While other animals bought the biggest homes they could get,
The Bears warned them to stay out of debt.
"Be grateful, work hard, and you'll find success,"
"A Bear can have more by living with less."

It wasn't until the farm had a drought,
The animals learned what the Bears warned about.
Without enough money to pay back the pigs,
Animals yelled, "The system is rigged."

Worm screamed, "Please don't take my home,"
"I promise I will pay back your loans!"
Grass, lights, stones, diamonds, urns, houses, and cribs,
All of it given, taken back by the Pigs.

Sloth could no longer lay around,
Worm could no longer live in the ground.
Rooster was left crying alone,
Lions were no longer able to roam.
Cow was left starving in hunger,
Chipmunk had to live with his blunder.

The Bears would have a big
celebration,
To enjoy the perks of
resisting temptation.
Family and friends
spent the day in the water,
They told the story of an
old Bear from Georgia.

"If the pigs come around pretending to care,"
Tell them, "I'm sorry,
but the market is Bear."

Write an Amazon Review ! ! !

Have you read
Good Bears Always Tell the Truth?

Made in United States
Orlando, FL
11 December 2024

55474181R00015